Three-Minute Tales

CHICKS

p

This is a Parragon book
This edition published in 2001

Parragon
Queen Street House, 4 Queen Street
Bath BA1 1HE, UK

Produced by The Templar Company plc
Pippbrook Mill, London Road, Dorking
Surrey RH4 1JE, UK

Edited by Caroline Repchuk
Designed by Kilnwood Graphics

Printed and bound in China
ISBN 0 75254 757 7

Three-Minute Tales

CHICKS

Written by Caroline Repchuk • Illustrated by Stephanie Boey

CONTENTS

Making A Splash!
Cheeky Chick

LITTLE CHICK LOST

"Stay close, Little Chick!" said Mummy,
as they set out to visit Mrs Duck, who lived
on the pond. Little Chick tried to keep up
with Mummy, but there were so many
interesting things to look at that he soon
got lost in the long grass.

He was busy watching a shiny beetle climb
a stem of grass, when a dark shadow fell
over him. Little Chick looked up to see a
huge dribbling mouth coming towards him!

It was a hungry fox! "Help!" he cried,
looking around for somewhere to hide.

Just then, Spot, the farm dog, appeared and
with a great woof he chased the fox away.
He was good at protecting the farm animals.
Mummy arrived flapping her wings.
"I told you to stay close," she said, tucking
Little Chick under her wing. And from then
on, that is just where Little Chick stayed!

THE DISAPPEARING EGGS

Mrs Hen had been sitting on her nest for
a long time, and she was tired and uncomfortable.
"I wish these eggs would hurry up and hatch!"
she said to herself, crossly. But all she could
do was sit and wait, so she closed her eyes
and soon fell fast asleep.

She dreamt she was sitting on her nest when all of a sudden it started to wobble and shake. She was tipped this way, and that, being poked and prodded as the eggs moved beneath her - someone was stealing her eggs! A deep voice was saying, "What lovely big ones!" It must be Mr Fox! She had to save her eggs!

Mrs Hen woke with a start, and looked down at her nest in alarm. Sure enough, her eggs had disappeared - but in their place were six fluffy chicks, all prodding her with their sharp little beaks.

"What lovely big ones!" said a deep voice
nearby. It was Old Ned, the donkey.
"Aren't they just!" said Mrs Hen with relief.
"They were certainly worth the wait!"

Making A Splash!

One day, Mrs Hen and her chicks were
walking near the pond, when Mrs Duck
swam by, followed by a line of ducklings.
The ducklings splashed around ducking
and diving in the water. "Can we play in
the water too?" the chicks asked Mrs Hen.
"It looks like fun!"

"Oh, no, dears," said Mrs Hen. "Chicks and water don't mix!" This made the chicks very miserable. "It's not fair!" they grumbled. "We wish we were ducklings!" On the way home, a big black cloud appeared and it started to rain. Soon the chicks' fluffy feathers were wet through.

They scurried back to the henhouse as
fast as they could and arrived wet, cold and
shivering. Soon they were snuggled in the
cosy warm straw, and
their feathers
were dry and
fluffy again.

"Imagine being wet all the time!" said the chicks. "Thank goodness we're not ducklings, after all!"

CHEEKY CHICK

Cheeky Chick was a playful little chick. He was always playing tricks on his brothers and sisters. He would hide in the long grass, then jump out on them in surprise, shouting, "Boo!" One day they decided to get their own back. "Let's play hide and seek," they said.

They left Cheeky Chick to count to ten,
while they all went to hide. Cheeky Chick
hunted high and low for his brothers
and sisters. He looked in all his favourite

hiding places but they were nowhere to be
found. "Come out," he called. "I give up!"
But no one came.

So Cheeky Chick carried on looking.
He searched carefully all through the
farmyard, through the vegetable patch and
along the hedgerow at the edge of the field.
He even looked in the haystack, which
took a very long time, but there was no sign
of his brothers and sisters to be found
amongst the hay.

By now it was getting dark, and Cheeky
Chick was feeling scared and lonely.
"It's no use," he said to himself. "I'll have
to go home." He hurried to the henhouse
and opened the door. "Surprise!" came
a loud chorus. His brothers and sisters
had been hiding there all along! It was
a long time before Cheeky Chick played
tricks on them again.

The End